Scarface Claw,
Hold Tight!

Lynley Dodd

PUFFIN

The morning was peaceful;
the birds in the trees
were fluffing their feathers
and teasing the bees.
Sunning himself
as he settled each paw
was lazy old sleepyhead,
Scarface Claw.

Suddenly,
there was a shudder and sway,
the whirr of an engine,
then off and away.
Down past the letter box,
no time to stop,
went Tom in a hurry –
WITH SCARFACE
ON TOP!

Out on the highway
they speedily sped,
past hedges and gates
and a tumbledown shed.
A battered old trailer
with four barking dogs,

a lumbering logging truck
loaded with logs.

Boys in a school bus
who hooted and whooped
while cows in a paddock
just nosily snooped.

Peter the plumber
tried waving a sock,

but Gran, on her scooter,
was shaking with shock.

Everyone pointed
and hollered and waved,
they hooted and tooted
and ranted and raved.
'HEY!' shouted Ray,
who was flapping his hat,
'SOMEBODY STOP HIM!'
and
'RESCUE THAT CAT!'

Constable Chrissie
was stunned at the sight;
she switched on her siren
and red and blue light.
'What a dilemma,
a difficult case!'
she said as she turned
for the rescuing
chase.

'Here's trouble,' said Tom,
'Not frolics and fun –
  but where is the problem
  and what have I done?'
  He jammed on his brakes
  and he slammed to a stop . . .

and Scarface went sliding
w-w-w-WHOOMPH
down
from
the
top.

Along came Miss Plum.
'Poor Scarface!' she said,
'You're muddled and fuddled
from wind in the head.'
With Constable Chrissie –
and plenty of luck –
she caught him
and bundled him
into the truck.

With whiskers a-bristle
and furious growls,
Scarface gave one
of his caterwaul yowls,
'YOW-OW-OW-EEOW!'
He glowered and scowled
with a crotchety groan
as Tom drove him –
double quick –

all the way

home.

PUFFIN BOOKS

UK | USA | Canada | Ireland | Australia | India | New Zealand | South Africa

Puffin Books is part of the Penguin Random House group of companies
whose addresses can be found at global.penguinrandomhouse.com.

www.penguin.co.uk   www.puffin.co.uk   www.ladybird.co.uk

First published by Penguin Random House New Zealand 2017
This edition published in Great Britain by Puffin Books 2019
001
Design by Cat Taylor © Penguin Random House New Zealand
Prepress by Image Centre Group
Printed and bound in China
A CIP catalogue record for this book is available from the British Library
ISBN: 978–0–241–34333–3
All correspondence to: Puffin Books, Penguin Random House Children's 80
Strand, London WC2R 0RL

MIX
Paper from
responsible sources
FSC® C018179
FSC
www.fsc.org